Perritos/Dogs

Labradores/ Labradors

por/by Connie Colwell Miller

Traducción/Translation: Dr. Martín Luis Guzmán Ferrer
Editor Consultor/Consulting Editor: Dra. Gail Saunders-Smith

Consultor/Consultant: Jennifer Zablotny, DVM
Member, American Veterinary Medical Association

Mankato, Minnesota

Pebble Books are published by Capstone Press,
151 Good Counsel Drive, P.O. Box 669, Mankato, Minnesota 56002.
www.capstonepress.com

Copyright © 2009 by Capstone Press, a Capstone Publishers company.
All rights reserved. No part of this publication may be reproduced in whole or in part, or stored in a retrieval system, or transmitted in any form or by any means, electronic, mechanical, photocopying, recording, or otherwise, without written permission of the publisher.
For information regarding permission, write to Capstone Press,
151 Good Counsel Drive, P.O. Box 669, Dept. R, Mankato, Minnesota 56002.
Printed in the United States of America

1 2 3 4 5 6 14 13 12 11 10 09

Library of Congress Cataloging-in-Publication Data
Miller, Connie Colwell, 1976–
 [Labradors. Spanish & English]
 Labradores = Labradors / por/by Connie Colwell Miller.
 p. cm. — (Pebble. Perritos = Dogs)
 Includes index.
 Summary: "Simple text and photographs present the Labrador breed and how to care for them — in both English and Spanish" — Provided by publisher.
 ISBN-13: 978-1-4296-3256-0 (hardcover)
 ISBN-10: 1-4296-3256-9 (hardcover)
 1. Labrador retriever — Juvenile literature. I. Title. II. Title: Labradors. III. Series.
SF429.L3M5518 2009
636.752'7 — dc22   2008034539

Note to Parents and Teachers

The Perritos/Dogs set supports national science standards related to life science. This book describes and illustrates Labradors in both English and Spanish. The images support early readers in understanding the text. The repetition of words and phrases helps early readers learn new words. This book also introduces early readers to subject-specific vocabulary words, which are defined in the Glossary section. Early readers may need assistance to read some words and to use the Table of Contents, Glossary, Internet Sites, and Index sections of the book.

Table of Contents

Loyal Labs 5
From Puppy to Adult 9
Taking Care of Labs 15
Glossary 22
Internet Sites 22
Index 24

Tabla de contenidos

Los leales labradores 5
De cachorro a adulto 9
Cómo cuidar al labrador 15
Glosario 23
Sitios de Internet 23
Índice 24

Loyal Labs

Labrador are friendly, loyal pets. People call them "Labs" for short.

Los leales labradores

Los labradores son unas mascotas cariñosas y leales. En Estados Unidos la gente les llaman "labs" para abreviar.

Some Labs are hunting dogs. They splash into the water to fetch ducks and geese.

Algunos labradores son perros de caza. Chapotean en el agua para cobrar patos o gansos.

From Puppy to Adult

Lab puppies love to play. They are gentle and friendly with kids.

De cachorro a adulto

A los cachorros labradores les encanta jugar. Son mansos y cariñosos con los niños.

Lab puppies can be black, chocolate brown, or yellow. Some puppy litters are all one color. Some litters are mixed.

Los cachorros labradores pueden ser negros, color chocolate o amarillos. Algunas camadas de cachorros son de un sólo color. Otras son una mezcla.

Adult Labs have strong bodies. Their short coats are waterproof. Their long tails and webbed toes help them swim.

Los labradores adultos tienen unos cuerpos fuertes. Su pelo es impermeable. Sus largas colas y los dedos de sus patas palmeadas los ayudan a nadar.

Taking Care of Labs

Labs are big dogs that need a lot of exercise. Owners should take Labs on long walks every day.

Cómo cuidar al labrador

Los labradores son perros grandes que necesitan mucho ejercicio. Los dueños de los labradores deben hacer largas caminatas con ellos todos los días.

Labs like lots of activity. Owners can train them for dog shows. Labs can learn to jump over bars and crawl through tunnels.

Al labrador le gusta mucho la actividad. Los dueños pueden entrenarlos para participar en concursos de perros. El labrador aprende a saltar obstáculos y arrastrarse por los túneles.

Labs' short coats are easy to care for. Owners should brush them once each week.

El pelo corto del labrador es muy fácil de cuidar. Su dueño debe cepillarlo una vez a la semana.

Labradors are popular dogs. When well cared for, they are playful pets for many years.

Los labradores son perros muy populares. Cuando están bien cuidados, son unas juguetonas mascotas que viven muchos años.

Glossary

dog show — a contest where judges pick the best dog in several events

litter — a group of animals born at the same time to one mother

waterproof — able to keep water out

webbed — having folds of skin that connect the toes

Internet Sites

FactHound offers a safe, fun way to find educator-approved Internet sites related to this book.

Here's what you do:

1. Visit *www.facthound.com*
2. Choose your grade level.
3. Begin your search.

This book's ID number is 9781429632560.

FactHound will fetch the best sites for you!

Glosario

la camada — grupo de recién nacidos que la hembra tiene al mismo tiempo

el concurso de perros — competencia donde los jueces escogen al mejor perro que participa en varios eventos

impermeable — capaz de impedir que entre el agua

palmeada — que tiene pliegues de piel que unen a los dedos

Sitios de Internet

FactHound te brinda una forma segura y divertida de encontrar sitios de Internet relacionados con este libro y aprobados por docentes.

Lo haces así:
1. Visita *www.facthound.com*
2. Selecciona tu grado escolar.
3. Comienza tu búsqueda.

El número de identificación de este libro es 9781429632560.

¡FactHound buscará los mejores sitios para ti!

Index

brushing, 19
coats, 13, 19
color, 11
dog shows, 17
exercise, 15
fetching, 7

hunting, 7
litters, 11
puppies, 9, 11
swimming, 13
tails, 13
walks, 15

Índice

cachorros, 9, 11
camada, 11
caminatas, 15
caza, 7
cepillar, 19
cobrar, 7

colas, 13
color, 11
concurso de perros, 17
ejercicio, 15
nadar, 13
pelo, 13, 19

Editorial Credits
Martha E. H. Rustad, editor; Katy Kudela, bilingual editor; Adalín Torres-Zayas, Spanish copy editor; Juliette Peters, designer; Kyle Grenz, book designer; Kara Birr, photo researcher; Scott Thoms, photo editor

Photo Credits
Ardea/Jean Michel Labat, 4; Capstone Press/Karon Dubke, 14, 18; Cheryl A. Ertelt, cover; Corbis/George D. Lepp, 10; Kent Dannen, 16; Lynn M. Stone, 6; Photo by Fiona Green, 20; Photodisc/Ryan McVay, 8; Shutterstock/Tina Rencelj, 1, 12